INVISIBLE STANLEY

By Jeff Brown
Illustrated by Steve Björkman

HarperTrophy®
A Division of HarperCollins Publishers

Harper Trophy® is a registered trademark
of HarperCollins Publishers Inc.

Invisible Stanley
Text copyright © 1996 by Jeff Brown
Illustrations copyright © 1996 by Steve Björkman
Printed in the U.S.A. All rights reserved.

Library of Congress Cataloging-in-Publication Data
Brown, Jeff, date
  Invisible Stanley / by Jeff Brown ; illustrated by Steve Björkman.
    p.   cm.
  Summary: One morning after a thunderstorm, the Lambchop family is sur-
prised to discover that Stanley is suddenly invisible.
  ISBN 0-06-442029-9
  [1. Brothers—Fiction. 2. Humorous Stories.] I. Björkman, Steve, ill. II.
Title.
PZ7.B81422In 1996   96-52
[Fic]—dc20   CIP
                                     AC

Typography by Alison Donalty

❖

First Edition

For Robert Brown
—J.B.

CONTENTS

Prologue 3

1 Where Is Stanley?....................7

2 Dr. Dan 13

3 The First Days.......................21

4 In the Park...........................27

5 The TV Show 39

6 The Bank Robbers 59

7 Arthur's Storm.......................71

INVISIBLE
STANLEY

Prologue

Stanley Lambchop spoke into the darkness above his bed. "I can't sleep. It's the rain, I think."

There was no response from the bed across the room.

"I'm hungry, too," Stanley said. "Are you awake, Arthur?"

"I am now," said his younger brother. "You woke me."

Stanley fetched an apple from the kitchen

and ate it by the bedroom window. The rain had worsened.

"I'm still hungry," he said.

"Raisins . . . shelf . . ." murmured Arthur, half asleep again.

Crash! came thunder. Lightning flashed.

Stanley found the little box of raisins on a shelf by the window. He ate one.

Crash! Flash!

Stanley ate more raisins.

Crash! Flash!

Arthur yawned. "Go to bed. You can't be hungry still."

"I'm not, actually." Stanley got back into bed. "But I feel sort of . . . oh, *different,* I guess."

He slept.

Chapter One

Where Is Stanley?

"Breakfast is ready, George. We must wake the boys," Mrs. Lambchop said to her husband.

Just then, Arthur Lambchop called from the bedroom he shared with his brother.

"Hey! Come here! Hey!"

Mr. and Mrs. Lambchop smiled, recalling another morning that had begun like this. An enormous bulletin board, they discovered, had fallen on Stanley during the night, leaving him unhurt but no more than half an inch thick.

And so he had remained until Arthur blew him round again, weeks later, with a bicycle pump.

"Hey!" The call came again. "Are you coming? Hey!"

Mrs. Lambchop held firm views about good manners and correct speech. "Hay is for horses, not people, Arthur," she said as they entered the bedroom. "As well you know."

"Excuse me," said Arthur. "The thing is, I can *hear* Stanley, but I can't *find* him!"

Mr. and Mrs. Lambchop looked about the room. A shape was visible beneath the covers of Stanley's bed, and the pillow was squashed down, as if a head rested upon it. But there was no head.

"Why are you staring?" The voice was Stanley's.

Smiling, Mr. Lambchop looked under the bed but saw only a pair of slippers and an old tennis ball. "Not here," he said.

Arthur put out a hand, exploring. "Ouch!" said Stanley's voice. "You poked my nose!"

Arthur gasped.

Mrs. Lambchop stepped forward. "If I may . . . ?" Gently, using both hands, she felt about.

A giggle rose from the bed. "That *tickles*!"

"Oh, my!" said Mrs. Lambchop.

She looked at Mr. Lambchop and he at her, as they had during past great surprises. Stanley's flatness had been the first of these. Another had come the evening they discovered a young genie, Prince Haraz, in the bedroom with Stanley and Arthur, who had accidentally summoned him from a lamp.

Mrs. Lambchop drew a deep breath. "We must face facts, George. Stanley is now invisible."

"You're *right*!" said a startled voice from the bed. "I can't see my feet! Or my pajamas!"

"Darndest thing I've ever seen," said Mr. Lambchop. "Or *not* seen, I should say. Try some other pajamas, Stanley."

Stanley got out of bed and put on different pajamas, but these too vanished, reappearing only when he took them off. It was the same with the shirt and trousers he tried on next.

"Gracious!" Mrs. Lambchop shook her head. "How are we to keep *track* of you, dear?"

"I know!" said Arthur. Untying a small red balloon, a party favor, that floated above his bed, he gave Stanley the string to hold. "Try this," he said.

The string vanished, but not the balloon.

"There!" said Mrs. Lambchop. "At least we can tell, approximately, where Stanley is. Now let's all have breakfast. Then, George, we must see what Dr. Dan makes of this."

Chapter Two

Dr. Dan

"What's that red balloon doing here?" asked Dr. Dan. "Well, never mind. Good morning, Mr. and Mrs. Lambchop. Something about Stanley, my nurse says. He's not been taken flat again?"

"No, no," said Mrs. Lambchop. "Stanley has remained round."

"They mostly do," said Dr. Dan. "Well, let's have the little fellow in."

"I am in," said Stanley, standing directly before him. "Holding the balloon."

"Ha, ha, Mr. Lambchop!" said Dr. Dan. "You are an excellent ventriloquist! But I see through your little joke!"

"What you see through," said Mr. Lambchop, "is Stanley."

"Beg pardon?" said Dr. Dan.

"Stanley became invisible during the night," Mrs. Lambchop explained. "We are quite unsettled by it."

"Head ache?" Dr. Dan asked Stanley's balloon. "Throat sore? Stomach upset?"

"I feel fine," Stanley said.

"I see. Hmmmm . . ." Dr. Dan shook his head. "Frankly, despite my long years of practice, I've not run into this before. But one of my excellent medical books, *Difficult and Peculiar Cases* by Dr. Franz Gemeister, may help."

He took a large book from the shelf behind him and looked into it.

"Ah! 'Disappearances,' page 134." He found the page. "Hmmmm . . . Not much here, I'm afraid. France, 1851: a Madame Poulenc vanished while eating bananas in the rain. Spain, 1923: the Gonzales twins, age eleven, became invisible after eating fruit salad. Lightning had been observed. The most recent case, in 1968, is Oombok, an Eskimo chief, last seen eating canned peaches during a blizzard."

Dr. Dan returned the book to the shelf.

"That's it," he said. "Gemeister suspects a connection between bad weather and fruit."

"It stormed last night," said Stanley. "And I ate an apple. Raisins, too."

"There you are," said Dr. Dan. "But we must look on the bright side, Mr. and Mrs. Lambchop. Stanley seems perfectly healthy, except for the visibility factor. We'll just keep an eye on him."

"Easier said than done," said Mr. Lambchop. "Why do his *clothes* also disappear?"

"Not my field, I'm afraid," said Dr. Dan. "I suggest a textile specialist."

"We've kept you long enough, Doctor," Mrs. Lambchop said. "Come, George, Stanley— Where *are* you, Stanley? Ah! Just hold the balloon a bit higher, dear. Good-bye, Dr. Dan."

By dinnertime Mr. and Mrs. Lambchop and Arthur had become quite sad. The red balloon, though useful in locating Stanley, kept reminding them of how much they missed his dear face and smile.

But after dinner Mrs. Lambchop, who was artistically talented, replaced the red balloon with a pretty white one and got out her water-color paints. Using four colors and several delicate brushes, she painted an excellent like-ness of Stanley, smiling, on the white balloon.

Everyone became at once more cheerful. Stanley said he felt almost his old self again, especially when he looked in the mirror.

Chapter Three

The First Days

The next morning Mrs. Lambchop wrote a note to Stanley's teacher, tied a stronger string to his balloon, and sent him off to school.

"Dear Miss Benchley," the note said. "Stanley has unexpectedly become invisible. You will find the balloon a useful guide to his presence. Sincerely, Harriet Lambchop."

Miss Benchley spoke to the class. "We must not stare at where we suppose Stanley to be," she said. "Or gossip about his state."

Nevertheless, word soon reached a newspaper. A reporter visited the school and his story appeared the next day.

The headline read: SMILING STUDENT: "ONCE YOU SAW HIM, NOW YOU DON'T!" Beneath it were two photographs, a Before and an After.

The Before, taken by Miss Benchley a week earlier, showed a smiling Stanley at his desk. The After, taken by the reporter, showed only Stanley's desk and his smiley-face balloon bobbing above it. The story included a statement by Miss Benchley that Stanley was

BEFORE

AFTER

in fact at the desk and, to the best of her knowl-
edge, smiling.

Mr. and Mrs. Lambchop bought several
copies of the paper for out-of-town friends. Her
colorful balloon artwork lost something in
black and white, Mrs. Lambchop said, but on
the whole it had photographed well.

Arthur said that "Invisible Boy's Brother"
would have been an interesting picture, and
that Stanley should suggest it if the reporter
came around again.

Being invisible offered temptations, Mr. and
Mrs. Lambchop warned, but Stanley must
resist them. It would be wrong to spy on
people, for example, or sneak up on them to
hear what they were saying.

But the next Saturday afternoon, when the Lambchops went to the movies, it was Arthur who could not resist.

"Don't buy a seat for Stanley," he whispered at the ticket window. "Just hide his balloon. Who'd know?"

"That would be deceitful, dear," said Mrs. Lambchop. "Four seats, please," she told the ticket lady. "We want one for our coats, you see."

"Wasn't *that* deceitful, sort of?" Arthur asked as they went in.

"Not in the same way," said Mr. Lambchop, tucking Stanley's balloon beneath his seat.

Just as the film began, a very tall man sat directly in front of Stanley, blocking his view. Mr. Lambchop took Stanley on his lap, from which the screen was easily seen, and the people farther back saw right through him without knowing it. Stanley greatly enjoyed the show.

"See?" said Arthur as they went out. "Stanley didn't even *need* a seat."

"You have a point," said Mr. Lambchop, whose legs had gone to sleep.

Chapter Four

In the Park

It was Sunday afternoon. Arthur had gone to visit a friend, so Mr. and Mrs. Lambchop set out with Stanley for a nearby park. The streets were crowded, and Stanley carried his balloon to lessen the risk of being jostled by people hurrying by.

Near the park they met Ralph Jones, an old college friend of Mr. Lambchop's.

"Always a treat running into your family, George!" said Mr. Jones. "The older boy was flat once, I recall. You had him rolled up. And once you had a foreign lad with you. A prince, yes?"

"What a memory you have!" said Mr. Lambchop, recalling the young genie who had been with them at the time.

"How are you, Ralph?" said Mrs. Lambchop. "Stanley? Say hello to Mr. Jones."

"Take care!" said Mr. Jones. "That balloon is floating—hmmmm . . . Just where *is* Stanley?"

"Holding the balloon," Stanley said. "I got invisible somehow."

"Is that so? First flat, now invisible." Ralph Jones shook his head. "Kids! Always one thing or another, eh, George? My oldest needs dental work. Well, I must run! Remember me to that prince. Prince Fawzi Mustafa Aslan Mirza Melek Namerd Haraz, as I recall."

"A truly *remarkable* memory," said Mrs. Lambchop as Mr. Jones walked away.

By a field in the park, the Lambchops found a bench on which to rest.

On the field, children were racing bicycles, round and round. Suddenly, shouts rose. "Give up, Billy! . . . Billy's no good! . . . Billy, Billy, silly Billy, he can't ride a bike!"

"That must be Billy," said Mrs. Lambchop. "The little fellow so far behind the rest. Oh, dear! How he teeters!"

Stanley remembered how nervous he had been when he was learning to ride and how his father had steadied him. Poor Billy! If only . . . I'll do it! he thought, and tied his balloon to the bench.

When Billy came round again, Stanley darted onto the field. Taking hold of the teetering bicycle from behind, he began to run.

"Uh-oh!" said little Billy, surprised to be gaining speed.

Stanley ran harder, keeping the bicycle steady. The pedals rose and fell, faster and faster, then faster still.

"Yikes!" cried Billy.

Stanley ran as fast as he could. Soon they passed the boy riding just ahead, then another boy and another! Not until they had passed all the other riders did Stanley, now out of breath, let go.

"Wheeee!" Billy shouted, and went round once more by himself.

"You win, Billy!" shouted the other boys. "How did you get so good? . . . And so *suddenly*! . . . You sure had us fooled!"

Stanley got his breath back and returned to Mr. and Mrs. Lambchop on the bench.

"Too bad you missed it, Stanley," said Mr. Lambchop, pretending he had not guessed the truth. "That teetery little boy—he rode very well suddenly."

"Oh?" said Stanley, pretending also. "I wasn't paying attention, I guess."

Mr. Lambchop gave him a little poke in the ribs.

Half an hour passed, and Mrs. Lambchop worried that they might be sitting too long in the sun. In Stanley's present state, she said, over-tanning would be difficult to detect.

Just then, a young man and a pretty girl strolled past, hand in hand, and halted in a grove of trees close by.

"That is Phillip, the son of my dear friend Mrs. Hodgson," Mrs. Lambchop said. "And the girl must be his sweetheart, Lucia. Such a sad story! They are in love and Phillip wants very much to propose marriage. But he is too shy. He tries and tries, Mrs. Hodgson says, but each time his courage fails. And Lucia is too timid to coax the proposal from him."

Mr. Lambchop was not the least bit shy. "I'll go introduce myself," he said. "And pop the question for him."

"No, George." Mrs. Lambchop shook her head. "Lucia must hear the words from Phillip's own lips."

An idea came to Stanley.

"Be right back!" he said, and ran to the grove in which the young couple stood. Once beside them, he stood very still.

". . . nice day, Lucia, don't you think?" Phillip was saying. "Though they say it may rain. Who knows?"

"You are quite right, I'm sure, Phillip," the girl replied. "I do value your opinions about the weather."

"You are kind, very kind." Phillip trembled a bit. "Lucia, I want to ask . . . I mean . . . Would you . . . Consent, that is . . ." He gulped. "What a pretty dress you have on!"

"Thank you," said Lucia. "I like your neck-tie. You were saying, Phillip?"

"Ah!" said Phillip. "Right! Yes! For some time now, dear Lucia . . . My dearest wish . . . Oh, my! I want . . ." He bit his lip. "Look! A dark cloud, there in the west! It may rain after all."

"I hope not." Lucia seemed close to tears. "I mean, if it rained . . . Well, we might get wet."

This is *very* boring, Stanley thought.

The conversation grew even more boring. Again and again Phillip failed to declare his love, chattering instead about the weather, or the look of a tree, or children playing in the park.

"I want to ask, dear Lucia," Phillip began again for perhaps the twentieth time, "if you will . . . That is . . . If you . . . If . . ."

"Yes?" said Lucia, also perhaps for the twentieth time. "*What,* Phillip? *What* do you wish to say?"

Stanley leaned forward.

"Lucia . . . ?" said Phillip. "Hmmm . . . Ah! I . . ."

"Marry me!" said Stanley, making his voice as much like Phillip's as he could.

Lucia's eyes opened wide. "I *will*, Phillip!" she cried. "Of course I will marry you!"

Phillip looked as if he might faint. "What? Did I—? You *will*?"

Lucia hugged him, and they kissed.

"I've proposed at last!" cried Phillip. "I can hardly believe I spoke the words!"

You didn't, Stanley thought.

Mr. and Mrs. Lambchop had seen the lovers embrace. "Well done, Stanley!" they said when he returned to their bench, and several more times on the way home.

Mrs. Hodgson called that evening to report that Phillip and Lucia would soon be wed. How wonderful! Mrs. Lambchop said. She had glimpsed them in the park just that afternoon. Such a handsome pair! So much in love!

Stanley teased her. "You said never to sneak up on people or spy on them. But I did today. Are you mad at me?"

"Oh, very angry," said Mrs. Lambchop, and kissed the top of his head.

Chapter Five

The TV Show

Arthur was feeling left out. "Stanley always gets to have interesting adventures," he said. "And that newspaper story was just about him. Nobody seems interested in me."

"The best way to draw attention, dear," said Mrs. Lambchop, "is by one's character. Be kindly. And fair. Cheerfulness is much admired, as is wit."

"I can't manage all that," said Arthur.

Mrs. Lambchop spoke privately to Stanley. "Your brother is a bit jealous," she said.

"When I was flat, Arthur was jealous because people stared at me," Stanley said. "Now they can't see me at all, and he's jealous again."

Mrs. Lambchop sighed. "If you can find a way to cheer him, do."

The very next day an important TV person telephoned Mr. Lambchop.

"Teddy Talker here, Lambchop," he said. "Host of the enormously popular TV show, *Talking with Teddy Talker*. Will Stanley appear on it?"

"It would please us to have Stanley *appear* anywhere at all," Mr. Lambchop said. "People can't see him, you know."

"I'll just say he's there," said Teddy Talker. "Speak to the boy. Let me know."

Stanley said that he did not particularly care to go on TV. But then he remembered about cheering up Arthur.

"All right," he said. "But Arthur, too. He likes to tell jokes and do magic tricks. Say we'll *both* be on the show."

Arthur was very pleased, and that evening the brothers planned what they would do. The next morning Mr. Lambchop told Teddy Talker.

"Excellent plan!" said the TV man. "This Friday, yes? Thank you, Lambchop!"

"Welcome, everybody!" said Teddy Talker that Friday evening from the stage of his TV show. "Wonderful guests tonight! Including an invisible boy!"

In the front row, applauding with the rest of the audience, Mr. and Mrs. Lambchop thought of Stanley and Arthur, now waiting in a dressing room backstage. How excited they must be!

The other guests were already seated on the sofa by Teddy Talker's desk. He chatted first with a lady who had written a book about sausage, next with a tennis champion who had become a rabbi, then with a very pretty young woman who had won a beauty contest, but planned now to devote herself to the cause of world peace.

At last came the announcement that began the Lambchop plan.

"Invisible Stanley has been delayed but will be here shortly," Teddy Talker told the audience. "Meanwhile, we are fortunate in having with us his very talented brother!"

Protests rose. "Brother? . . . A *visible* brother? . . . Drat! . . . Good thing we got in free!"

"Ladies and gentlemen!" said Teddy Talker. "Mirth and magic with Arthur Lambchop!"

Arthur stepped out onto the stage wearing a smart black magician's cape Mrs. Lambchop had made for him and carrying a small box, which he placed on Teddy Talker's desk.

"Hello, everybody!" he said. "The box is for later. Now let's have fun! Heard the story about the three holes in the ground?" He waited, smiling. "Well, well, well!"

Two people laughed, but that was all.

"I don't understand," said a lady sitting

behind Mr. and Mrs. Lambchop.

Mr. Lambchop turned around in his seat. "A 'well' is a hole in the ground," he said. " 'Well, well, well.' Three holes."

"Ah! I see!" said the lady.

"A riddle, ladies and gentlemen!" cried Arthur. "Where do kings keep their armies?"

"Where?" someone called.

"In their sleevies!" said Arthur.

Many people laughed now, including the lady who had missed the first joke. "I got that one," she said.

"A mind-reading trick!" Arthur announced. He shuffled a deck of cards and let Teddy Talker draw one.

"Don't let me see it!" he said. "But look at it! Picture it in your mind! I will concentrate, using my magic powers!" Arthur closed his eyes. "Hmmm . . . hmmm . . . Your card, sir, is the four of hearts!"

"It is!" cried Teddy Talker. "It *is* the four of hearts!"

Voices rose again. "Incredible! . . . He can read minds? . . . So young, too! . . . Do that one again, lad!"

"Certainly!" said Arthur.

But he had used a false deck in which *every* card was the four of hearts, and the audience would surely guess if that card was named again. Fortunately, the brothers had thought of this. Backstage, Stanley tied his balloon to a chair.

Arthur now shuffled a real deck of cards, then called for a volunteer. When an elderly gentleman came up onto the stage, Stanley tiptoed out to stand behind him. The audience applauded the volunteer. How peculiar this is! Stanley thought. Hundreds of people looking, but not one can see me!

"Draw a card, sir!" said Arthur. "Thank you! Keep it hidden! But picture it in your mind!" Again closing his eyes, he pretended to be thinking hard.

A quick peek showed Stanley that the volunteer held the ten of clubs. He tiptoed over to whisper in his brother's ear.

Arthur opened his eyes. "I have it. The card is . . . the ten of clubs!"

"Yes! Bravo!" cried the old gentleman. The audience clapped hard as he returned to his seat.

Mr. Lambchop smiled at the lady behind him. "Our son," he said.

"So clever!" said the lady. "What *will* he do next?"

Mrs. Lambchop drew a deep breath. That morning Stanley and Arthur had borrowed a pet frog from the boy next door. What came next, she knew, would be the most daring part of the evening's plan!

"Ladies and gentlemen!" said Arthur. "A new kind of magic! Arthur Lambchop—that's me!—and Henry, the Air-Dancing Frog!"

He lifted Henry from the box on Teddy Talker's desk and held him up. Henry, who appeared to be smiling, wore a little white shirt with an H on it, also made by Mrs. Lambchop.

"Fly, Henry!" cried Arthur. "Fly out and stand still in the air!"

Stepping forward, Stanley took Henry from Arthur's hands and ran to the far side of the stage. There he stopped, holding the frog high above his head. Henry wriggled his legs.

"Amazing!" shouted the audience. "Who'd believe it? . . . That's some frog! . . . What keeps him up there?"

"Circle, Henry!" Arthur commanded. "Circle in the air!"

Stanley walked rapidly in circles, swaying Henry as he went.

The audience was tremendously impressed. "What a fine magician! . . . Mind reading *and* frog flying! . . . You don't see that every day!"

Pretending to control Henry's flight, Arthur kept a finger pointed as Stanley swooped the frog all about the stage. "Whoops!" cried Teddy Talker as Henry flew above his desk. On the long sofa, the sausage writer and the tennis rabbi and the beauty-contest winner ducked down. Even Mr. and Mrs. Lambchop, who knew the secret of Henry's flight, thought it an amazing sight.

At last, to great applause, Arthur took Henry into his own hands and returned him to the little box.

Stanley tiptoed off to get his smiley-face balloon. The plan now called for Teddy Talker

to announce the arrival of the invisible boy and introduce him.

But Arthur had stepped forward again.

"Thank you for cheering me," he told the audience. "But I have to say something. That first mind-reading trick, I really did do that one. But the second trick . . . Actually, I can't read minds at all. And the flying frog, he—"

Voices rose. "Can't read minds? . . . We've been lied to? . . . The *frog* was lying? . . . Not the frog, stupid! . . . Wait, he's not done!"

"Please! Listen!" said Arthur. "It wouldn't be fair to let you think I did everything by myself. I had a helper! For the second trick, he saw the card and told me what it was. And Henry . . . Well, my helper was whooshing him in the air!"

By now the audience was terribly confused. "Who? . . . What helper? . . . It was just a regular frog? . . . But *some* frogs fly! . . . No, squirrels, not frogs! . . . *Whooshing?*"

Arthur went on. "My brother Stanley helped me! He fixed it for me to be on this show! He's a really nice brother, and I thank him a lot!"

Teddy Talker had sprung to his feet. "Ladies and gentlemen! May I now present a very special guest, who has been here all along! The invisible boy! Stanley Lambchop!"

Stanley came onto the stage, carrying his smiley-face balloon. Arthur put out his hand, and the audience could tell that Stanley had taken it. There was tremendous applause.

The brothers bowed again and again,

Stanley's balloon bobbing up and down. Arthur's smile was plain to see, and Mr. and Mrs. Lambchop, as they applauded, thought that even the balloon's painted smile seemed brighter than before.

"I have two children myself," said the lady behind them. "Both entirely visible and without theatrical flair. We are a very *usual* family."

"As are we," said Mr. Lambchop, smiling. "Mostly, that is."

Arthur left the stage, and Stanley sat on the sofa between the sausage writer and the beauty-contest winner and answered Teddy Talker's questions. He had no idea *how* he became invisible, he said, and it wasn't actually a great treat being that way, since he often got bumped into and had to keep reminding people he was there. After that, Teddy Talker thanked everyone for coming, and the show was over.

Back home, Arthur felt the evening had gone well.

"I got lots of applause," he said. "But maybe it was mostly because of what Stanley did. I shouldn't be too proud, I guess."

"Poise and good humor contribute greatly to a performer's success," said Mrs. Lambchop. "You did well on both those counts. Return Henry in the morning, dear. Time now for bed."

Chapter Six

The Bank Robbers

Mr. Lambchop and Stanley and Arthur were watching the evening news on TV.

". . . more dreadful scandal and violence tomorrow," said the newscaster, ending a report on national affairs. "Here in our fair city another bank was robbed today, the third this month. The unusual robbers—"

"Enough of crime!" Bustling in, Mrs. Lambchop switched off the TV. "Come to dinner!"

Stanley supposed he would never know

how the robbers were unusual. But the next afternoon, while strolling with his father, he found out. On the way home they passed a bank.

"I must cash a check, but it is very crowded in there," said Mr. Lambchop. "Wait here, Stanley."

Stanley waited.

Suddenly, cries rose from within the bank. "Lady bank robbers! Just like they said on TV! . . . I laughed when I heard it! . . . Me, too!"

Two women in dresses and fancy hats, one stout and the other very tall, ran out of the bank, each with a money bag in one hand and a pistol in the other.

"Stay in there!" the stout woman called back into the bank, her voice high and scratchy. "Don't anyone run out! Or else . . . Bang! Bang!"

"Right!" shouted the tall woman, also in an odd, high voice. "Just because we are females doesn't mean we can't shoot!"

Being invisible won't protect me if bullets go flying about! Stanley thought. He looked for a place to hide.

An empty Yum-Yum ice cream van was parked close by and he jumped into it. His balloon still floated outside the van, its string caught in the door, but he did not dare to rescue it. Scrunching down behind cardboard barrels marked CHOCOLATE YUM, STRAWBERRY YUM, and YUM CRUNCH, he peeked out.

An alarm was ringing inside the bank, and shouts rose again. "Ha! Now you're in trouble! . . . The police will come! . . . Put that money back where you found it, ladies!"

Then Stanley saw that the two robber women were running toward him, carrying the money bags. They were stopping! They were getting into the Yum-Yum van!

Scrunching down again, he held his breath.

The robbers were in the van now, close to where he hid. "Hurry up!" said the stout woman in a surprisingly deep voice. "These shoes are killing me!"

The tall woman opened the YUM CRUNCH barrel, and Stanley saw that it was empty. Then both robbers poured packets of money from their bags into the barrel and put the lid back on.

Stanley could hardly believe what he saw next!

The robbers threw aside their fancy hats and tugged off wigs. And now they were undressing, pulling their dresses over their heads!

They were *men,* Stanley realized, not women! Yes! Underneath the dresses they wore white ice-cream-man pants, with the legs rolled up, and white Yum-Yum shirts!

"Whew! What a relief, Howard!" The stout robber kicked off his women's shoes and put on white sneakers.

"They'll never catch us now, Ralph!" said the tall one.

The robbers unrolled their trouser legs and threw their female clothing into another empty barrel, the one marked CHOCOLATE YUM. Then they jumped into the front seats, the tall man driving, and the van sped off.

Behind the barrels, Stanley held his breath again. This pair was too clever to be caught! They were sure to get away! No one would suspect two Yum-Yum men of being the lady— But the van was slowing! It was stopping!

Stanley peeked out again.

A police car blocked the road and two policemen stood beside it, inspecting cars as they passed by. In a moment they were at the Yum-Yum van.

"A bank got robbed," the first policeman told the driver. "By two women. You ice cream fellows seen any suspicious-looking females?"

"My!" The tall man shook his head. "More and more these days, women filling roles once played by men. Bless 'em, I say!"

Beside him, the stout man said hastily, "But

bank robbing, Howard, that's *wrong*."

The second policeman looked into the back of the van. "Just ice cream here," he told his partner.

The trickery is working! Stanley thought. How can I . . . ? An idea came to him. Reaching out, he flipped the lid off the CHOCOLATE YUM barrel.

"Loose lid," said the second policeman. "Better tighten— Hey! This barrel is full of female clothes!"

"Oh!" The tall robber made a sad face. "For the needy," he said. "They were my late mother's."

Stanley flipped the lid off the YUM CRUNCH barrel and the packets of money were plain to see!

"Your mother was a mighty rich woman!" shouted the first policeman, drawing his pistol. "Hands up, you two!"

As the robbers were being handcuffed, another police car drove up. Mr. Lambchop jumped out of it.

"That balloon, on that van!" he shouted. "We've been following it! Stanley . . . ? Are you in there?"

"Yes!" Stanley called back. "I'm fine. The bank robbers are caught! They weren't ladies at all, just dressed that way!"

The handcuffed robbers were dreadfully confused. "Who's yelling in our van? . . . Who stuck a balloon in the door? . . . Have we gone crazy?" they asked.

"It's my son Stanley," said Mr. Lambchop. "He is invisible, unfortunately. Thank goodness he was not hurt!"

"That must be the same invisible boy they had on TV!" said the first policeman.

"An invisible boy?" The tall robber groaned. "After all my careful planning!"

The stout robber shrugged. "You can't think of *everything,* Howard. Don't blame yourself."

The robbers were driven off to jail, and Stanley went home with Mr. Lambchop in a cab.

Stanley had been far too brave, Mrs. Lambchop said when she heard what he had done. Really! Flipping those ice cream lids! Arthur said he'd have flipped them too, if he'd thought of it.

Chapter Seven

Arthur's Storm

Mr. and Mrs. Lambchop had said good night. For a moment the brothers lay silent in their beds.

Then Arthur yawned. "Good night, Stanley. Pleasant dreams."

"Pleasant dreams? Hah!"

"Hah?"

"Those robbers today, they had *guns*!" said Stanley. "They could have shot me by accident and nobody would even know."

"I never thought of that." Arthur sat up. "Are you mad at me?"

"I guess not. But . . ." Stanley sighed. "The thing is, I don't want to go on being invisible. I was really scared today, and I hate carrying that balloon, but when I don't, people bump into me. And I can't see myself in the mirror, so I don't even remember how I look! It's like when I was flat. It was all right for a while, but then people laughed at me."

"That's why I blew you round again," Arthur said proudly. "Everyone said how smart I was."

"If you're so smart, get me out of *this* fix!" There was a little tremble in Stanley's voice.

Arthur went to sit on the edge of his brother's bed. Feeling for a foot beneath the covers, he patted it. "I'm really sorry for you," he said. "I wish—"

There was a knock at the door, and Mr. and Mrs. Lambchop came in. "Talking, you two? You ought to be asleep," they said.

Arthur explained about Stanley's unhappiness.

"There's more," Stanley said. "Twice my friends had parties and didn't invite me. They sometimes forget me even if I *do* keep waving that balloon!"

"Poor dear!" Mrs. Lambchop said. " 'Out of sight, out of mind,' as the saying goes." She went to put her arms around Stanley, but he had just sat up in bed and she missed him. She found him and gave him a hug.

"This is awful!" Arthur said. "We have to *do* something!"

Mr. Lambchop shook his head. "Dr. Dan

knew of no cure for Stanley's condition. And little about its cause except for a possible connection between bad weather and fruit."

"Then I'll always be like this." Stanley's voice trembled again. "I'll get older and bigger, but no one will ever see."

Arthur was thinking. "Stanley did eat fruit. And there *was* a storm. Maybe . . . Wait!"

He explained his idea.

Mr. and Mrs. Lambchop looked at each other, then at where they supposed Stanley to be, and at each other again.

"I'm not afraid," said Stanley. "Let's *try*!"

Mr. Lambchop nodded. "I see no harm in it."

"Nor I," said Mrs. Lambchop. "Very well, Arthur! Let us gather what your plan requires!"

"Everyone ready?" said Arthur. "It has to be just the way it was the night Stanley got invisible."

"I'm wearing the same blue-and-white stripey pajamas," said Stanley. "And I have an apple. And a box of raisins."

"We can't make a real storm," Arthur said. "But maybe this will work."

He stepped into the bathroom and ran the water in the sink and shower. "There's rain," he said, returning. "I'll be wind."

Mrs. Lambchop held up a wooden spoon and a large skillet from the kitchen. "Thunder ready," she said.

Mr. Lambchop showed the powerful flashlight he had fetched from his tool kit. "Lightning ready."

Stanley raised his apple. "Now?"

"Go stand by the window," said Arthur. "Now let me think. Hmmm . . . It was dark." He put out the light. "Go on, eat. *Whooosh!*" he added, being wind.

Stanley began to eat the apple.

Water pattered down in the bathroom, into the sink and from the shower into the tub.

"Whoooosh . . . whooosh!" said Arthur, and Mrs. Lambchop struck her skillet with the wooden spoon. The *crash!* was much like thunder.

"Lightning, please," Arthur said.

Mr. Lambchop aimed his flashlight and flicked it on and off while Stanley finished the apple.

"Now the raisins," said Arthur. "One at a time. *Whooosh!*"

Stanley opened the little box and ate a raisin.

Still *whoooosh*ing, Arthur conducted as if an orchestra sat before him. His left hand signaled Mrs. Lambchop to strike the skillet, the right one Mr. Lambchop to flash the light. Nods told Stanley when to eat a raisin.

Patter . . . splash went the water in the bathroom. *"Whooosh!"* went Arthur. *Crash!* went the skillet. *Flash! . . . Flash!* went the light.

"If anyone should see us now," Mrs. Lambchop said softly, "I would be hard put to explain."

Stanley looked down at himself. "It's no use," he said. "I'm still invisible."

"Twist around!" said Arthur. "Maybe the noise and light have to hit you just a certain way!"

Twisting, Stanley ate three more raisins. The light flickered over him. He heard the water splashing, Arthur *whooosh*ing, the pounding of the skillet with the spoon. How hard they were trying, he thought. How much he loved them all!

But he was still invisible.

"There's only one raisin left," he said. "It's no use."

"Poor Stanley!" cried Mrs. Lambchop.

Arthur could not bear the thought of never seeing his brother again. "Do the last raisin, Stanley," he said. "Do it!"

Stanley ate the raisin and did one more twist. Mrs. Lambchop tapped her skillet and Mr. Lambchop flashed his light. Arthur gave a last *Whooosh!*

Nothing happened.

"At least I'm not hungry," Stanley said bravely. "But—" He put a hand to his cheek. "I feel . . . sort of tingly."

"Stanley!" said Mr. Lambchop. "Are you touching your cheek? I see your hand, I think!"

"And your pajamas!" shouted Arthur, switching on the light.

A sort of outline of Stanley Lambchop, with hazy stripes running up and down it, had appeared by the window. Through the stripes they could see the house next door.

Suddenly the outline filled in. There stood Stanley in his striped pajamas, just as they remembered him!

"I can see my feet!" Stanley shouted. "It's *me*!"

"*I*, dear, not *me*," said Mrs. Lambchop before she could catch herself, then ran to hold him tight.

Mr. Lambchop shook hands with Arthur, and then they all went into the bathroom to watch Stanley look at himself in the mirror.

It hadn't mattered when he was invisible, Mrs. Lambchop said, but he was greatly in need of a haircut now.

She made hot chocolate to celebrate the occasion, and Arthur's cleverness was acknowledged by all.

"But false storms cannot be relied upon," Mr. Lambchop said. "We must think twice before eating fruit during bad weather. Especially by a window."

Then the brothers were tucked into bed again. "Good night," said Mr. and Mrs. Lambchop, putting out the light.

"Good night," said Stanley and Arthur.

Stanley got up and went to have another look in the bathroom mirror. "Thank you, Arthur," he said, coming back. "You saved me from being flat, and now you've saved me again."

"Oh, well . . ." Arthur yawned. "Stanley? Try to stay, you know, *regular* for a while."

"I will," said Stanley.

Soon they were both asleep.